# THE SEVEN VOYAGES OF
# SINBAD THE SAILOR

# THE SEVEN VOYAGES OF SINBAD THE SAILOR

## ILLUSTRATED BY QUENTIN BLAKE

RETOLD BY
# JOHN YEOMAN

Margaret K. McElderry Books

This version of *The Voyages of Sinbad the Sailor* has been written by John Yeoman from existing translations.

**MARGARET K. McELDERRY BOOKS**
25 YEARS • 1972–1997

Margaret K. McElderry Books
An imprint of Simon & Schuster Children's Publishing Division
1230 Avenue of the Americas
New York, New York 10020

Designed by Bernard Higton.
The text of this book is set in Simoncini Garamond.
The illustrations were done in line and watercolor.

Printed and bound in Spain by Bookprint

10 9 8 7 6 5 4 3 2 1

Library of Congress Catalog Card Number: 96-77400

ISBN 0-689-81368-6

# CONTENTS

\* \* \*

# FOREWORD

THE stories about Sinbad come from that huge collection of Middle Eastern tales called *The Arabian Nights* or, sometimes, *The Thousand and One Nights*. It is in that collection that we can also find other well-known stories such as *Aladdin* and *Ali Baba and the Forty Thieves*. These stories have been famous for a long time. They were first translated into French, and then almost immediately into English, over two hundred years ago; but the stories themselves were first told hundreds of years before that.

Sinbad himself has been so well known in English for such a long time that most people have heard of him. "Sinbad the Sailor" is easy to say and it sounds right, but what we notice when we come to read these stories is that Sinbad isn't really a *sailor*—he's a merchant and, most importantly, a traveller. One almost wants to say that his special achievement is *getting shipwrecked*. Perhaps that isn't so surprising, since the conditions of travel in those days were truly hazardous. The Sinbad stories (unlike the others in *The Arabian Nights*) must be based on the yarns that the real travellers of that time told on their return. No doubt some such accounts would have got confused in the telling. When you come across the rhinoceros in this book you'll find that the storyteller has got its appearance about right, but some of its habits—lifting an elephant on its horn, for instance—hopelessly wrong. And of course, as there were no photographs, no film cameras, and precious few other witnesses, there was nothing to stop the returning merchant exaggerating to make his adventures even more impressive.

Isn't this what we find so attractive about these stories—that, though they are so extraordinary, there is in them somewhere an element of truth? (Just as I was doing my pictures of the Roc I met someone who told me that in Madagascar there are traces of bones of birds far larger that any we have seen...)

There's a warm wind blowing across the eastern seas. Shall we set sail once again with Sinbad?

*Quentin Blake*

# THE STORY OF SINBAD THE SAILOR

IN Baghdad, during the reign of the Calif, Harun al-Rashid, there lived a poor man called Sinbad the Porter who earned his living by carrying bundles on his head. One hot day, when he was sweating under a particularly heavy load, he found himself passing the gate of a merchant's house where the ground had been swept and freshened with water and the air smelled sweet. Spotting a bench beside the courtyard door, he set his load down and decided to have a rest and breathe in the delicious smells.

He perched himself on the edge of the bench and suddenly became aware of all kinds of fascinating sounds coming from within: voices singing and reciting, lutes and other instruments playing, and thrushes and nightingales warbling away.

He thought this was so wonderful that he couldn't resist tiptoeing to the gate and peering round. There before him was an enormous garden filled with pages and slaves and all manner of servants and attendants such as you only find in the grandest palaces. And the air was scented with the aromas of the richest and most delicate dishes and of the choicest wines.

And he fell to thinking how strange it was that Fortune gives some people a life of luxury, while others have to sweat and slave for very little. Without realizing what he was doing, he broke into a little song that he'd invented:

"There's some that's born to pass their days
 In having fun in different ways.
They play the lute, and dance, and dine,
And sing their songs, and drink their wine.
While others hardly rest at all;
Like me, they're at men's beck and call."

When he had finished his song he heaved his bundle back on his head and was about to set off again when a smartly dressed little page popped out through the gateway.

"Be so good as to come in with me," he said, "for my master wishes to see you."

Sinbad the Porter was so embarrassed by this invitation that he blurted out a lot of excuses, but the young page wouldn't take "No" for an answer. So he left his load at the gatekeeper's lodge and followed the boy into the house, which he discovered to be a vast, brightly lit mansion. He was led into a grand hall where a company of noble people was assembled, feasting off the most sumptuous food and wine imaginable, to the accompaniment of wonderful music. Everyone was seated in order of rank, and at the highest place of all sat a majestic and dignified man with streaks of grey in his beard.

Sinbad the Porter could hardly take it all in. "This must either be Heaven or a king's palace," he said to himself.

Then he suddenly remembered his duty and flung himself to his knees before the master of the house, bowing his head to the floor.

"Pray rise and be seated," said the master, patting the cushion by his side, "and join us in our feast." At this he clapped his hands, and servants came running with more rich and delicious dishes than Sinbad the Porter had ever seen in his life. He praised his host with all his heart and set to.

When he could eat no more and had washed his fingers in the finger-bowl he nodded respectfully to the company and thanked his host again.

"You are most welcome," said his host, smiling. "But you haven't yet told us your name and what you do for a living."

"My name, sir, is Sinbad, and I work as a porter, hiring myself out to carry folks' bundles on my head."

"What a happy coincidence," said the master, "for my name is Sinbad too: Sinbad the Sailor. And now I should consider it a great pleasure if you would sing for us the song that you were singing at my gates."

Sinbad the Porter grew very embarrassed, and stammered that his host might find the words rather impertinent, being such a rich and distinguished man.

"Not at all," said Sinbad the Sailor. "The song pleased me when you first sang it, and anyway, we have become brothers now."

So Sinbad the Porter sang his song again and the master of the house listened to it with a look of great satisfaction on his face.

When he had finished, his host said, "I can imagine that you have had a difficult life, but you must know that I had to undergo many trials before I became the lord of this place. I have made seven voyages in my life, and in each of them I had an amazing adventure. My good lords," he said, turning to address his guests, "I shall now tell you the story of The First Voyage of Sinbad the Sailor."

\* \* \*

# THE
# FIRST VOYAGE

## OF SINBAD THE SAILOR

My father, who was a very rich merchant, died when I was still a child, leaving me enormous wealth and property and land. When I became a young man and could get my hands on the money, I spent and spent on expensive clothes and fine living, treating all my friends to the very best of everything—as if the money would last forever. But finally I came to my senses and realized that if I carried on in this way I should soon be facing poverty.

So I resolved to do something about it. I sold my remaining possessions and fine clothes for three thousand dirhams, enough to fund me for a journey to foreign parts. And with the money I bought some goods to trade with and all I needed for a long voyage, and joined a company of merchants on board a vessel bound for Basra, where we changed ship. At first I suffered terribly from seasickness, but I quickly got over it and, since then, I've never been bothered by it again. We sailed for weeks on end, travelling through the Persian Gulf and into the Arabian Sea, going from island to island, buying and selling and bartering wherever we put into port, until finally we reached an island that looked just like the gardens of Paradise.

We cast anchor and landed, and in no time we were busying ourselves in our different ways: making ovens in the sand, cooking, washing, exploring, and playing games to amuse ourselves. At one point I thought I felt a small earth tremor, but nobody else seemed to notice it. They just carried on with what they were doing. I went off with a small group to explore, but we hadn't ventured very far before we heard the ship's captain hailing us from the gunwale at the top of his voice.

"Run for your lives!" he was calling. "Drop everything and get back on board. This isn't an island, after all. We've landed on a monstrous fish that's been asleep so long that the sands have settled over it and the trees have sprung up on it. But when you lit your fires it felt the heat and began to stir. At any moment it will plunge down into the depths, taking you all with it. Get back to the ship before you drown!"

We didn't need any persuading, I can tell you. We abandoned our bundles of merchandise, our spare clothes, our cooking pots, and·everything else in our mad scramble back to the ship. Some of them made it: I was one of those who didn't.

For, suddenly, the island gave an almighty shudder and plunged into the depths. I thought I was finished as the crashing waves closed over my head but, as luck would have it, I was swept against a great wooden trough which I reached out for and clung to for dear life. Finally I managed to get astride it, paddling with my feet, while the waves buffeted me this way and that.

Meanwhile, the captain, who must have believed we were drowned, set sail. I watched the vessel disappear over the horizon and gave myself up for lost. All that night and most of the next day the tossing waves bore me along until the trough was washed up against the steep banks of a wooded island. Grabbing hold of an overhanging branch, I was able to hoist myself onto dry land.

Up to this moment I had only felt fear and exhaustion, but now sensation was returning. My legs were seized with cramp, and the soles of my feet were stinging where they had been bitten by fish.

I collapsed on the ground, more in a stupor than in sleep, and lay there until the next day's sun revived me. My feet were still

horribly tender, but I found that I could crawl on my knees or shuffle about on my backside to find fruit and sweet spring water.

Little by little my strength began to return and my spirits began to revive. When I could walk comfortably again, using a stick that I cut from a tree, I decided to explore the island. On one of my expeditions I caught sight of some animal in the distance moving about at the water's edge. At first I thought it must be a wild beast or perhaps even a sea monster, but as I cautiously drew nearer I could make out that it was a horse: a magnificent mare, tethered to a log on the beach.

I decided to approach her, but as I put out my hand she reared up and whinnied so loudly that I stumbled back in fear and turned to run. But as I did so a man burst out from under the ground and stopped me, demanding to know who I was and what I was doing there.

"Oh, good sir," I said, "I am but a stranger thrown up on these shores by Fortune when my fellow-travellers perished at sea." Hearing this, he took me by the hand and motioned me to go with him. To my surprise he led me down to an underground chamber the size of a great hall.

He sat me down at the upper end and put some food in front of me. While I was eating my fill he gently plied me with questions about myself until, finally, I had told him everything that had happened to me since I had set sail. He was amazed and could hardly believe that it was true.

It was then my turn to question him. "And now, good sir," I said, "kindly tell me who you are, and why you live beneath the earth, and why you tether such a fine mare at the water's edge."

"I am one of the grooms of King Mihrjan," he said. "We are stationed in various places across this island, and we have sole charge of the king's horses. Every month, at about the time of the new moon, we bring some of our best young mares, tether them on the seashore, and hide ourselves beneath the ground, waiting for the sea-stallions. Soon the stallions catch the scent of the mares and, seeing no one, emerge from the sea to mate with them. But then they try to entice the mares away with them, into the waves, and it is then that we must leap from our hiding places, shouting and waving our arms, in order to startle the stallions and drive them back into the sea.

"When the mares finally give birth to their foals, the little creatures are worth their weight in gold. There are no other horses like them on the face of the earth. And now," he said, "it is time for me to report to our great King Mihrjan. You are indeed fortunate that you stumbled upon us, for I shall be the means not only of saving your life but of returning you to your own land."

After this we sat talking for a while until the other grooms arrived for their meal. They were all curious to know how I came to be among them and so I repeated my story while they ate.

Then it was time to set off for the palace. They on their steeds and I on one of the mares they had provided for me, we rode nonstop until we reached the gates of the capital city of King Mihrjan. We dismounted in the grand courtyard, where my host told me to wait while he acquainted the king with my story.

Shortly after I was summoned into the royal presence. The King greeted me courteously and, wishing me a long life, desired me to tell him my tale in my own words. So once again I told my story in every detail.

The King was most impressed. "My son," he said, "you are clearly blessed by Fortune, and while you remain with us you shall be well treated and well rewarded." And then, to my astonishment, he appointed me as his agent for the port. My main job would be to register all the ships that entered the port.

I told him how deeply grateful I was and accepted the post with thanks. My work necessitated reporting to the King regularly, and he became even more considerate towards me with the passing of time. From his hands I received all kinds of costly gifts, and soon I became a trusted intermediary between the King and any of his subjects who wanted to petition him.

For a long time I enjoyed my new responsibilities, but all the same I never lost the opportunity of questioning the merchants

and sailors and travellers who put into port about their travels, in the hope of hearing some news of Baghdad. But, sadly, I never found anyone who knew my native city or who knew of anyone who planned to sail there.

For all the ease and comfort of my new life as the King's agent, I was becoming homesick. But I soldiered on, making the best of things, paying frequent trips to the islands of King Mihrjan's dominions to take my mind off home. Among the remarkable things that I encountered were the Island of Kasil, where mysterious drumbeats are heard all through the night; and a monster fish some two hundred cubits long that is much feared by fishermen, who strike together pieces of wood to frighten it off. I also saw another fish that had the head of an owl, besides many other fantastic things that I haven't time to tell you of now.

And then, one day, a new ship sailed into the port. While the sailors were putting out the gangplanks and unloading the cargo, I stood making my notes as usual. Finally I asked the master whether there was any other merchandise left on board to add to my list.

"All that remain, my lord," he replied, "are certain bundles of goods that belonged to a merchant who was drowned during our voyage. I intend to sell them and give the money to his people in Baghdad when we return there."

My heart missed a beat. "What was this merchant's name?" I asked.

When he said "Sinbad the Sailor," I immediately recognized him, and let out a great cry of joy. "I am that very Sinbad the Sailor," I said, "who disappeared beneath the waves when the great fish heaved, and would have drowned had it not been for a wooden tub that Fortune cast my way." And I told him my story and how I had come to be the King's overseer of the port. "So you see, good sir," I said, "this merchandise you speak of is mine."

The master lifted his eyes to the heavens and exclaimed, "Is there no honesty left in this wicked world!"

I couldn't believe my ears. "What can you mean?" I asked. "You surely don't disbelieve me?"

"I told you the story of this misfortune," he said, "and you saw a way of getting your hands on the goods. Of course I don't believe you: I saw the wretched man drown before my very eyes."

I had to tell him in great detail everything that had happened on board after we left Baghdad and everything that we had done on the fish-island before I could convince him of the truth.

"You are truly blessed by Fortune," he said, apologizing for his doubts. And he gave orders for all my bales to be handed over to me.

At once I made up a collection of the finest and costliest items, hired some of the sailors to carry it for me, and took it to the palace to present it to the King, who was delighted with the gift and even more delighted with my good luck.

Then I traded the remaining goods for a handsome profit and bought some of the local wares for a very reasonable cost. When the time came for the ship to set sail, I went back to the King and requested his permission to return home with it. He wished me well and generously bestowed more luxurious presents upon me.

The homeward voyage, I am pleased to say, was uneventful. On reaching Baghdad I made straight for my house. When news of my arrival reached my kinsfolk and friends, they immediately came to greet me. In no time I had engaged servants and was able to entertain even more generously than I had done previously. I soon forgot the hardships and dangers and loneliness of my travels, and sank once more into a life of ease.

And that is the story of my first voyage. Tomorrow I shall tell you the story of my second.

\* \* \*

Then Sinbad the Sailor gave Sinbad the Porter a hundred gold dinars, and told him how much his presence had cheered the company.

Sinbad the Porter thanked his host kindly and went on his way, marvelling at the remarkable events that had just been recounted to him.

Early the next morning he returned to the house of Sinbad the Sailor and was once again greeted warmly and made to sit by his host's side. When the distinguished company had assembled and everyone had feasted well, they were treated to the story of The Second Voyage of Sinbad the Sailor.

# THE
# SECOND VOYAGE

## OF SÎNBAD THE SAILOR

I WAS leading a highly enjoyable life until one day I was suddenly seized with a longing to travel the world again, and to make myself another fortune by trading. And so I took a great purse of gold and bought myself a wealth of merchandise and everything I needed for my voyage, and had it all bundled up in great bales.

Then I went down to the port and found a gleaming new ship that was just about to leave. She was an impressive vessel with sails made of fine cloth, and she had a first-class crew. Together with some other merchants, I arranged my passage with the captain, and on that very same day our goods were embarked and we set sail.

Once again I was excited by the life of travel and commerce. We had a remarkably smooth voyage, sailing from city to city and island to island. Everywhere we landed we were greeted by throngs of distinguished lords and merchants who were eager to barter and trade with us.

At last Destiny brought us to an island that was rich in heavily laden fruit trees and heavily scented plants, with no sound but the gentle warbling of the birds and the murmur of the streams. Nowhere was there any sign of human habitation.

As soon as we had dropped anchor all the sailors and the merchants, myself included, went ashore to enjoy the wonderful greenness of the place. I found myself a spot by a spring of cool water that welled up among the trees and sat down to a meal of the provisions I had brought with me. The breeze was so sweet with the fragrance of all the flowers that, soon after I had finished, I became drowsy and drifted off into a deep sleep.

When I finally awoke the sun was just beginning to set. To my surprise I seemed alone; there was no sign of the crew or my fellow merchants. The ship had gone, and no one had given a thought for me!

In despair, I searched the length and breadth of the little island, knowing that my search was futile. And, indeed, it proved what I knew already: I was totally alone.

I beat my breast in misery and cursed myself for having tempted Fate by venturing on a second voyage when it was only by good fortune that I had survived the first. To think that I could have been in my own house in Baghdad, surrounded by my friends, enjoying the best of food and wines with them. And here I was, through my own folly, left to finish my days in utter solitude.

I was so distressed that I blundered around the island like a madman. I climbed a tall tree in the desperate hope of seeing signs of human life, but there was nothing but vegetation and sand and sea and sky.

But just as I was about to make my descent I spotted something glistening white in the far distance. Once down from the tree I collected the rest of my provisions and set out to investigate. It took some time to reach it, but at last I found myself near enough to make out that it was an enormous white globe. It had no openings of any kind on its rounded sides, and it was far too smooth and curved for me to be able to climb up and examine the top. By walking around it I was able to discover that it was fifty paces in circumference.

While I was puzzling over what it could be and how it came to be there, the sunset sky suddenly turned black. At first I thought that a thick cloud must have appeared, but then I realized that a gigantic bird was winging its way towards me and blotting out the sun as it approached.

I immediately recalled the travellers' tales of the great Roc, the bird that is famed for feeding its young on elephants, and knew that this must be it and that the white globe must be its egg.

Taking shelter among some fronds, I saw the Roc land on the egg and settle with its wings around it protectively and its legs stretched out behind it. Very quietly I crept out from my hiding place and, with trembling hands, unwrapped my turban. Twisting it like a rope, I bound it tightly around my waist and tied the ends around one of the Roc's legs. It didn't move.

My idea was that, on its flight for food the following morning, it would carry me with it and take me within reach of my fellow men. I can tell you, I didn't sleep a wink that night for fear that the powerful bird might suddenly take off and catch me unawares.

As dawn approached the Roc began to stir and preen itself, and then, with a great screech, it launched itself into the air with me, eyes tightly shut, clinging grimly to my turban rope. The Roc swooped and soared until I almost lost consciousness, but finally I felt it making a gentle descent and landing.

As soon as my feet made contact with the solid ground, I wasted no time in releasing myself from its leg and diving behind a boulder for cover. But at no time had the great creature shown any awareness of my presence: I must have felt no heavier than a feather.

All the same, it was all I could do to stop myself from shaking, and I breathed a deep sigh of relief when I saw it bound forward, seize something in its claws, and rise into the air. To my amazement, I realized that it was clutching an enormous serpent.

Despite the size and strength of the great reptile, it writhed helplessly in the iron grip of the Roc as it was borne out of sight.

I suddenly became aware that the Roc had left me on a ledge overlooking a deep valley that was surrounded on all sides by towering mountains, far too steep for a man to climb. Once again I had reason to curse my stupidity. At least the island would have provided me with nourishing fruits to eat and fresh water to drink, whereas I was certain to starve to death in this barren wilderness.

Clambering down to the floor of the valley in the hope of finding at least some plants to eat, I was amazed to find that the

stones that lay scattered all around were, in fact, diamonds—
some of a truly astonishing size. This discovery distracted my
mind from my plight for some time, until I became aware of yet
another cause for alarm. There, immediately ahead of me, I saw
that the caves of the valley were heaving with serpents so gigantic
that the very smallest of them could have swallowed an elephant
without difficulty. I reasoned, correctly as it turned out, that

during the daylight hours they concealed themselves from the Roc
and the immense eagles that circled high overhead, but I knew
that the valley would not be a safe place for me at night.

And so, when the sun began to set, I found myself a narrow
opening in the rock face and squeezed through, closing the hole
behind me with a stone that was just big enough to fill the gap
while still letting in a little light. When my eyes grew accustomed
to the dim light, my heart nearly failed. At the far end of the
narrow cave lay a serpent, coiled around her eggs.

I had no choice but to remain in the cave all night, for I could
hear the constant hissing of the serpents searching for food
outside; but I scarcely closed my eyes for sheer terror. As soon as

daylight showed through the crack of the entrance I rolled back the stone and staggered out into the valley, faint with fear and fatigue and hunger.

It was while I was stumbling along in this dazed state that a slaughtered sheep came hurtling through the air and crashed down just in front of me. At first I was too amazed to be able to make any sense of what was happening, and then I remembered the stories I had heard of how diamond merchants are said to collect their stones in inaccessible places. They cut the throat of a sheep and skin it, and then they throw it down into the valley. The force with which the carcass strikes the ground causes the diamonds to stick to it. The hungry eagles and vultures quickly spot the bloody meat, swoop down upon it, and carry it up to the mountain summits with the gems still embedded in it.

Then the merchants emerge from their hiding places among the boulders and, banging sticks and shouting, scare the birds into abandoning their prey. All the merchants have to do then is to wrench the diamonds out of the flesh.

Weak and light-headed though I was, I quickly realized that this was my one hope of rescue. Hurriedly filling my pockets, my provisions bag, and the folds of my clothes with the largest diamonds that were scattered around, I lay down on my back, hauled the carcass on top of me, and bound myself to it with my unwound turban. In no time at all an eagle swooped down on the sheep and seized it in its talons. I found myself being lifted high into the air, all the while clinging on for dear life and not daring to look down.

The breath was knocked out of me when the eagle reached the summit and dropped the carcass, in preparation for ripping it to

shreds. Luckily for me the travellers' tales that I had heard proved to be the truth. A great clattering of wooden sticks and a frenzied shouting sent the bird flapping away from its meal, leaving me free to release myself from under the dead sheep.

The merchant who came running up turned pale with horror as he saw me emerge, my clothes all bloodstained, from under the meat. But his fear gave way to dismay when he summoned up enough courage to turn the carcass over and found nothing clinging to it.

I hastened to reassure him. "Believe me," I said, "I, too, am a merchant, and an honest man. I have about me more diamonds, and diamonds of far greater value, than you have ever seen together before. You shall have enough of them to make your fortune."

At this he thanked and blessed me, and summoned all the other merchants who were hiding among the rocks, waiting for their carcasses to be returned.

We passed that night together in a safe place that they had found, and they listened with wonder at my story of how I had been abandoned on the island and how I had reached the valley.

The first merchant declared that I must be truly fortunate. "Because," he said, "no man has ever been known to emerge alive from the Valley of the Serpents." And they all congratulated me on my safe deliverance.

The next morning they escorted me through a pass in the mountain range, from where I got frequent glimpses of the giant serpents in the valley below to remind me of my lucky escape. Finally we descended to a port and crossed to the Island of Roha.

There I was shown a plantation of camphor trees so immense that a hundred men could take shelter under any one of them. The natives collect the camphor by boring into the upper part of the trunk with a long iron rod, causing the liquid camphor—the sap of the tree—to run down the tree into vessels, in which it sets like gum. After this the tree dies and is used for firewood.

Another remarkable feature of this island is the rhinoceros, a huge creature with a horn on its forehead ten cubits long that reveals the likeness of a man when it is cut in half. Travellers tell that this beast, which the natives call "karkadan," is strong enough to carry off an elephant spiked on its horn, while it peacefully grazes on the leaves and twigs it finds along the coast. However, the elephant finally dies, and the fat of it, melting in the sun, runs down into the rhinoceros's eyes, blinding it and causing it to lie down on the shore. This makes it an easy prey for the giant Roc, which comes swooping down to carry off the rhinoceros, elephant and all, to feed to its young.

My companions introduced me to local merchants who

exchanged some of my diamonds for gold and silver, and then we journeyed on from country to country and town to town, all the while trading and bartering, until I finally arrived back home in Baghdad with a great store of diamonds and money and precious goods.

I was able to make gifts to all my friends, and resumed my former life of entertaining lavishly. Although I was frequently begged to recount the details of my remarkable adventures, the comforts of my new life made me soon forget the sufferings I had endured on my travels.

And that is the story of my second voyage. Tomorrow I shall tell you the story of my third.

\* \* \*

Then, when they had feasted to their hearts' content, Sinbad the Sailor presented Sinbad the Porter with a hundred gold dinars, for which the Porter thanked him profusely—and had still not finished thanking him by the time he reached home that night.

The next day he returned to the merchant's house, as he had been bidden, and when the assembled company was once more in a festive mood, they were treated to the story of The Third Voyage of Sinbad the Sailor.

# THE
# THIRD VOYAGE

# OF SINBAD THE SAILOR

FOR a while I relished my even greater prosperity and ease until, at last, the old thirst for travel, adventure, and material gain (for we are all weak creatures) made me restless once more.

I made up my mind immediately, bought up a plentiful quantity of trading stock, equipped myself for a long sea voyage, and set off for the port of Basra. Once again I found a fine ship ready to sail. It had a full crew and had attracted a good company of prosperous and distinguished merchants who welcomed me among their ranks.

The voyage began well. We visited some marvellous lands, and everywhere we dropped anchor my fortunes flourished. But one ill-fated day, as if from nowhere, a mighty storm arose and our sturdy ship was buffeted and tossed by the dashing waves. Suddenly we heard the voice of the ship's master above the roaring sea. He was on the gunwale, straining his eyes for the sight of dry land.

"Alas," he cried, "the wind has got the better of us and has driven us off course into mid-ocean. And Destiny, or ill-luck, is casting us upon the shore below the Mountain of the Zughb tribe, a hairy folk that are like apes, from whom no man ever escaped alive. Fall to your prayers, my friends, for soon we shall all be dead!"

Eventually we found ourselves in slightly calmer waters. But our relief was short-lived: almost at once we spotted a crowd of the ape-like creatures bearing down upon us. They were a revolting sight, with black faces and little yellow eyes, and their bodies were covered in ginger hair that was like felt. Although they were small, only four spans in height, we were afraid to strike them or try to drive them away because there were so many of them swarming

along the shore and splashing through the water. We feared that if we hurt one, the rest would set upon us in their fury. And so we just had to stay still and watch them clambering over the ship and leaping among the cables and the ship's ropes and gnawing them apart, causing the ship to swing around helplessly in the wind.

What was even more frightening was that they seized hold of every one of us and manhandled us to the shore. And then, mercifully, they swarmed back aboard to sail off in the lurching ship with all our goods.

At least we were alive, and the place proved to be well stocked with fruits and pot-herbs and fresh drinking water. And since there was no sign of the ape-like creatures we ventured a little further every day in our exploration of the island.

One day we made out, from the crest of a hill, what looked to be a large building in the middle of the island. We lost no time in making our way towards it, hoping to find help and protection there.

As we drew nearer, we were surprised to find that it was a vast ramshackle castle within a huge stockade, the great ebony doors of which stood wide open. We entered cautiously and found ourselves within an empty courtyard, at one end of which was a long stone bench and some braziers with cooking utensils and heaps of bones lying around.

As there was no one about, and the sun was hot, and we were exhausted after our trek through the undergrowth, we all lay down in the shade of a wall and quickly fell asleep.

It was sundown when we were startled awake by the earth trembling beneath us. You can imagine our horror as we saw, emerging from the castle, a giant-like creature with a swarthy complexion, huge shoulders, one single eye like a burning red coal, teeth like a boar's tusks, and a cavernous mouth. What's more, his lower lip hung down like a camel's over his chest, his ears flopped over his shoulders like an elephant's, and his fingernails were like a lion's claws. I nearly passed out at the sight of him.

He made no sound at first but merely slouched to the stone bench and sat himself down, looking at us attentively. Then, after sizing us up for a while, he got to his feet, came towards us, and

lifted me up for closer inspection. Turning me over in his hands,
he felt me as a cook feels a chicken he is about to choose for the
pot. Fate was on my side once more: he clearly thought me too
lean and stringy and knew he could do better. He picked up other
of my comrades in turn until he hit upon the solid form of the
ship's master.

An ugly smile showed us that the monster was well pleased with
his choice. He revived the fire in the brazier and put him on to
roast like a kebab. Having eaten his grim meal, he stretched
himself out on the stone bench and fell asleep.

His snoring was animal-like and disgusting, and it kept us
awake and in terror all night. It was not until he had slouched off

the following morning that we dared to say a word to each other. On one thing we were agreed: that it would have been better to have perished in the storm or to have been savaged to death by the ape-men than to be roasted alive by the giant—for that was sure to be the fate of each and every one of us, sooner or later.

Despite our fear, we dared to venture into the surrounding bushes in the hope of finding a hiding place. But nowhere offered good enough concealment, and we thought it wiser to return to the stockade as the sun began to set.

Soon the shuddering earth told us that the ogre was returning. It was just as before: he examined a few of us before choosing the plumpest, and then proceeded to roast him and eat him. When he was safely snoring again we became a little bolder, knowing now how deeply he slept, and whispered among ourselves.

Some of the merchants could only weep and bewail their misfortune, but I felt desperate enough to suggest a plan.

"My friends," I said, "rather than submit meekly to this horrible death by roasting alive, let us at least try to save ourselves. Only by killing the giant can we escape that fate. In this courtyard there are plenty of planks and pieces of rope. Tomorrow let us take them down to the shore and make some rafts for ourselves. If we succeed in killing the giant, we shall need to put to sea, either to let Fate take us to another shore or to put ourselves in the way of a passing ship that might save us. If we fail in our attempt to kill the giant, at least we might hope to run to the rafts and put ourselves beyond his reach."

It was agreed that anything was better than going like lambs to the slaughter. By the time the giant returned the following evening, we had constructed our rafts at the water's edge and had returned to the stockade, where we stuck one of the spits through the side of the brazier to get it burning hot.

The giant again took one of our wretched group for his supper and stretched himself out for his sleep on the bench. When his thunderous snores told us that he was well and truly unconscious, we all crept over to the brazier and carefully drew out the spit, which was now red-hot. Swinging it backwards and forwards to get our aim, we finally plunged it into his single red-rimmed eye, rendering him stone-blind on the spot.

He rose up in pain and panic, letting out a great cry that was enough to stop my heart beating for a moment. We scattered in all directions while he groped his way across the yard. His hands found the great gates and pushed them open, bursting the bolts. Then he stumbled out into the thicket, still howling.

We lost no time in scurrying down to the shore as best we could, hoping against hope that we would be safe until morning. But a quaking of the earth beneath our feet soon told us that we were far from safe. From a high rock, one of our number called out that the blinded giant was being led in our direction by two other one-eyed giants, each more hideous than he, at which we took to our rafts and paddled out as far as we could.

But the fellow giants caught sight of us and collected enormous boulders that they started throwing at us. Some fell harmlessly to one side, others made waves that rocked our flimsy rafts danger-ously, and yet others sank the slower rafts and drowned their crews.

When we had paddled far enough to be out of range of the rocks, I looked around me and realized that the few of us on our

raft were the only ones to have escaped. And that was not the end of our troubles, for as the relentless seas pounded us all through that night and the following days, others of our company died and had to be thrown into the waters.

By the time the waves had cast our raft onto another shore, there were only three of us left.

We dragged ourselves through the shallows, weak with fatigue and fear and hunger, and managed to reach a little stream where we bathed our faces and slaked our thirst. We also took a little of the abundance of fresh fruit that lay around, but our eyes were so weary and our bodies felt so heavy from sheer exhaustion that we quickly dropped off into a deep sleep.

I was soon roused from my disturbed dreams by a dreadful hissing sound in my ears. Opening my eyes with a start, I was horrified to see that we were encircled by the body of the most enormous dragon-like serpent. Its swollen belly heaved and its nostrils twitched as it eyed each of us in turn. At last it reared its head and struck out at one of my companions, seizing the unfortunate man's head in its jaws. It gulped him down slowly, bit by bit, until he had completely disappeared.

I shut my eyes tight and thought how wretched a creature I was, having escaped death at the hands of the giant and then by drowning, only to have the life crushed out of me in the gullet of a serpent.

But it seemed that the serpent was no longer hungry and, with a parting hiss, it simply lowered its huge head and slithered off into the undergrowth to digest its meal. Overcome with grief for our friend and fear for ourselves, my remaining companion and I scuttled off as fast as our trembling limbs would take us, and sought safety in the topmost boughs of a tall tree.

We were far from safe, however. I was shortly after awakened by the shaking of the branches caused by my companion's frenzied attempts to escape the serpent's hungry jaws. But the creature had already taken a firm grip on his head, and when it had swallowed him whole, it slithered down the tree and off into the darkness.

I passed the rest of the night in fear and trembling. When dawn broke I could see no sign of the serpent. I came down from the tree and climbed a high rock overlooking the sea, debating whether or not to throw myself in and put an end to it all. But I could not bring myself to do it.

If I could not end my life, then I had a duty to preserve it. Noticing some large pieces of wood scattered along the shore, I collected them together with some lengths of tough creeper. With some difficulty, I lay down on my back and contrived to tie a piece of wood across the soles of my feet, a piece along either side of me, a piece across the top of my head, and a piece like a lid on top of me. By this means I made a sort of box for myself as impregnable as the strongest oak chest.

The serpent returned that night, as I had supposed it would, and I watched with dread through the chinks of my wooden fortress as it circled around, trying in vain to fit the sharp angles of my box into its gaping jaws. All night it slithered around me, hissing and spitting as its disappointment and fury mounted. My heart didn't stop pounding until the dawn broke and it slunk back to its lair.

After a long struggle I was able to untie the last knot and release the wooden panels and free myself once more. Again I made for the high rock, where I stretched my limbs to restore the feeling to my numb body. I was musing on the wretchedness of the existence that lay ahead of me when I caught sight of a ship out at sea. With a strength that I didn't know I possessed, I ripped a long branch from a tree and waved it wildly above my head, calling out in a loud voice all the while.

Those on deck saw me and sent out a little boat to pick me up, more dead than alive. When they had given me a little to drink and to eat to restore my spirits, and had changed my filthy, salt-stained rags for some decent garments, they begged me to tell them how I had come to find myself alone on the island.

I recounted all my adventures from first to last, which caused great wonder and amazement you can be sure.

The ship continued its journey, with a fair wind, until it reached the island called Al-Salahitah, which abounds in sandalwood. There the captain cast anchor and the merchants landed with their goods to sell and barter.

"Because you are a stranger and a guest, and a man who has suffered many misfortunes," said the captain, "I have a mind to do something for you that will help you on your way back to your native land, where I hope I shall have your blessings."

"If you can do anything to help me back to my homeland, you can be assured of my continual blessings," I said, "for to return home is my dearest wish."

"I must explain," said the captain, "that when we set out on this voyage there was with us a rich merchant who later disappeared. Whether he is alive or dead I do not know, for we have had no news of him. I propose to entrust all his merchandise to your charge for you to trade with as you think fit. A proportion of the proceeds will be yours in reward for your efforts; the rest we shall keep until we return to Baghdad, when I shall search out his family."

"That is a most fair and generous offer," I said, "and I shall be most happy to perform this service to the best of my ability."

At this, the captain gave orders for the goods to be carried ashore for me, and he accompanied me to the wharf to see them unloaded and checked. "If you please, master," said the ship's scribe, "in whose name am I to list these items?"

"They must be put down as the merchandise of Sinbad the Sailor, whom we lost on the Island of the Roc, but now entrusted to this stranger to sell on commission on behalf of Sinbad's family."

I could scarcely believe my ears. Regarding the captain closely, I could indeed recognize him as the ship's master who had left me behind on the Island of the Roc, though he was very much changed. I realized that I, too, must have changed.

"Know, captain," I declared, "that I am that same Sinbad the Sailor, left behind when your ship sailed from the Island of the

Roc, and still alive and well after many an adventure. These goods are my goods; and these bales are my bales. All the merchants who fetch gems from the Valley of the Serpents will testify to my name, for I told them how I had been left behind and all that had befallen me since."

I was anxious at first because some of the passengers and crew were reluctant to believe me and suspected that I had designs on the dead Sinbad's goods. But Fortune was on my side once more, for among the crowd on the wharf was a merchant who, having heard mention of the Valley of the Serpents, had approached to hear the end of my story.

"My friends, I know this man," he said. "I told you the most remarkable thing that had happened to me in the Valley of the Serpents, when I hauled up a carcass to find a man, and not diamonds, clinging to it; this is that same man. And he gave me diamonds of greater value than I ever hoped to possess, and I accompanied him to Basra where he separated from us, telling us that his name was Sinbad the Sailor of Baghdad. I know him. And I know him to be a man of his word."

After hearing this, the captain was ready to believe me, but first he asked, "What was the special mark on your bales?" So I took a stick and drew the mark in the dust, which convinced him absolutely. He flung his arms around my neck and wished me joy.

After that I disposed of my long-lost merchandise very profitably and had good reason to congratulate myself not only on my safe deliverance from the many dangers of the voyage, but on my continuing prosperity.

Moreover, the rest of the journey gave me plentiful opportunities for further trade. In the lands of Hind and Sind I bought cloves and ginger and all kinds of exotic spices. These Indian seas afforded us countless wonders. We saw a cow-like fish that suckled its young; its hide is so tough that shields are made of it. There were also other fishes like asses and camels, and tortoises with shells twenty cubits across. And I saw a bird that lives in a seashell and comes to the surface to lay her eggs and hatch her chicks.

When we finally reached Basra, I bid my companions farewell and rested there a few days before returning to my family and friends in Baghdad. So rich had this voyage made me that I gave freely to relieve the sufferings of the widows and orphans of the city, and gave lavish feasts for all my old acquaintances.

And that is the story of my third voyage. Tomorrow I shall tell you the story of my fourth.

\* \* \*

Then Sinbad the Sailor presented Sinbad the Porter with yet another purse of a hundred gold dinars and called for more food and wine. That night, in his own house, Sinbad the Porter lay marvelling over the tales he had heard.

He could scarcely wait until dawn broke before making his way back to join the assembled guests to hear the story of The Fourth Voyage of Sinbad the Sailor.

# THE
# FOURTH VOYAGE

## OF SINBAD THE SAILOR

For a time after my return I lived in ease and comfort, surrounded by my good friends, and quite forgot the hardships that I had undergone in order to amass my fortune.

But one day I was visited by a company of merchants whom I invited to sit down and dine. They entertained us all with their talk of foreign travel and trade until my old restless self was stirred with new visions of adventure. I longed once more to visit foreign shores and sell my merchandise among strange peoples.

So I resolved to travel with them on their next voyage, and bought myself a stock of goods even more costly than before. We journeyed to Basra and at once set off, with a following wind and high hopes.

We sailed from island to island and sea to sea until one day, without warning, there arose a contrary wind that forced the captain to cast out his anchors, bringing the ship to a standstill.

As we fell to our prayers, there arose a fierce squall that, ripping the rigging to shreds and snapping the anchor cables, swept everyone overboard—goods and all. For half a day I kept myself alive by swimming, but found my strength failing at the end. And then, praise be, a long plank of wood from the broken-up ship came floating by. Together with some of the other merchants who were swimming alongside me, I clambered astride the plank as one might straddle a horse, and we paddled with our feet as best we could.

On the morning of the second day the turbulent sea flung us up on a beach, more dead than alive through exhaustion and want of food. We were fortunate enough to find some vegetation to nibble to sustain our failing strength before we all collapsed into a deep sleep.

The following morning we set out to explore the island, hoping to find some signs of human habitation. Our spirits were lifted when we saw what looked like some kind of dwelling in the distance. As we shuffled towards it, a number of naked men came out of the door and, without saluting us or greeting us in any way, laid hold of us and forced us inside.

There we found ourselves in the presence of their king, who motioned us to sit.

Then dishes of food were set before us, food such as I had never seen before in all my life. Hungry though I was, I was suspicious and held back, but my starving companions eagerly began to eat.

The more they ate, the more ravenously hungry they seemed to become, while our naked captors watched them with satisfaction. My companions were slowly losing their reason and beginning to act like beasts rather than men.

The naked men gave them coconut oil to drink and also rubbed it into their skin, which had the effect of making them even more animal-like. I feared for my poor friends, but I also feared for myself, even though the savages were taking little notice of me.

Then I recalled a traveller's tale that I had heard long ago and realized that this must be the tribe of the Magian cannibals. Every stranger to their shore is captured and led before the King. There he is fed upon that special food and anointed with that special oil, which increases his appetite until he becomes unnaturally fat and gross. At the same time he totally loses his reason. When he is considered ready, he is selected for the King and roasted. I was horrified at this thought, but powerless to help either my companions or myself.

We were led out of the room and entrusted to a kind of herdsman who put us out to pasture like so many cattle.

For days I existed on the small amount of leaves and berries and roots that my palate would accept, while my companions blissfully cropped the vegetation for hours on end, growing plumper and plumper by the day.

The naked men clearly had little interest in me, for the present, in my wasted state, and I found that I had the freedom to range further and further without attracting their attention. One day, when I feared that my friends were soon to be killed, I decided to try to escape.

I slipped away through the bushes and soon found myself within sight of another meadow where another herdsman was keeping watch over a similar wretched flock of men. Spotting me from afar, and realizing that I still possessed my reason, he gestured to me with an outstretched arm, as if to say, "Turn back, and take the right-hand path!"

This I gratefully did, running when I had the strength and taking frequent rests whenever I became weak with exhaustion.

For seven days and nights I followed that track, feeding only on handfuls of herbs and grasses.

It was not until the morning of the eighth day that I caught sight of other human beings. It was a group of men gathering pepper berries, and I watched them a long time from a distance before summoning up the courage to approach them.

As I stumbled forward they ran to greet me and questioned me about my weak state. When I explained, as best I could, about my experiences among the naked cannibals and about the plight of my former companions, they commiserated with me and begged me to accept meat and drink from their provisions.

They sat me down in the shade, and one of them told me how fortunate I had been to run away from the cannibals, as no man, once captured, had ever escaped their clutches.

I rested while they completed their day's work, and then they gently roused me and led me down to where their ship was moored. Then we set sail for their island home.

I was immediately taken before their king, who greeted me with
great courtesy and bade me sit by him and tell him of all my
adventures. He listened, enraptured, as I told my tales, and
ordered the finest dishes to be set before me.

Finally, he begged me to treat the city as my native city and the
palace as my home, for which I thanked him profusely. At his
invitation I wandered about the city, which was rich and popu-
lous, observing how busy and prosperous the tradespeople all
seemed to be.

I at once felt at home there, and every day after that would
spend much time walking about and making friends with all the
townsfolk until, little by little, I found myself one of the most
respected members of the community.

One curious thing that I observed was that all the citizens, high and low, rode fine thoroughbred horses, but that nowhere was there a saddle or trappings to be seen.

Much puzzled by this, I one day asked the King, "My lord, why is it that you choose to ride without a saddle?"

"A saddle?" he repeated. "What is a saddle? I do not know such a thing."

"With your permission," I said, "I will make you a saddle so that you may see for yourself exactly what benefits it brings."

"Do it with all my heart," said the King. "And command any of my faithful artisans to lend you whatever help and whatever materials you need."

So I sought a skilled carpenter who provided me with a fine block of wood from which he fashioned a saddle-tree from some drawings that I made him. Then I took some wool and teased it into felt. I covered the saddle-tree with leather that I then stuffed

with the felt, after which I polished it carefully and attached the girth and stirrup leathers. After that I got a blacksmith to make the stirrups and the bridle-bit according to my instructions, and then I fastened fringes of silk to the stirrups and fitted bridle leathers to the bit.

When all was completed to my satisfaction, I called for one of the finest of the royal horses to be brought to me and, having saddled and bridled him, led him into the presence of the King.

He was overjoyed by the splendid appearance of the horse and mounted him with great pleasure, cantering around the courtyard to the admiration of the assembled nobility.

When the King's wazir saw this he begged me, as a special kindness, to make him a similar one, which I did. Within days all the
grandees and the officers of state were requesting their own
saddles, and soon I had trained a band of skilled craftsmen work-
ing under my instructions to produce elegant saddles for the
whole court. I was showered with gold from my grateful
customers and by this means not only amassed a fortune but rose
in importance in the eyes of the King and his household.

One day the King surprised me as we reclined after a delicious
feast by asking me to make him a solemn promise. I was taken
aback and desired respectfully to know what the promise was.

"It is my wish," he said, "to marry you to a beautiful, intelli-
gent, and good-natured wife, so that you will truly think of this as
your home and dwell forever among us. I assure you that this is a
woman of good family who is as wealthy as she is fair. Surely you
could not find it in your heart to refuse me in this matter?"

To be honest, I was too confused to be able to utter a word.
"You are silent," said the King. "Have you nothing to say?"

"My master," I replied, "it is for you to command."

Thereupon he summoned the judge and the witnesses and
married me straight away to this lady of noble rank and pedigree.
In addition, he announced that he was presenting me with a
grand residence, together with a large retinue of servants and officers to be maintained at his own expense.

My wife and I fell deeply in love with each other, and I began to
enjoy life as never before. "When I return to my native land," I
vowed to myself, "I shall take my wife with me."

How little do we know what is in store for us. The two of us
lived in peace and absolute contentment for a great while until,

one day, I heard of the sad death of the wife of one of the courtiers.

Now this man was a great friend of mine and so I made for his house with all speed in order to offer him my condolences and to comfort him.

Finding him in great distress, I sought to console him by saying, "Do not grieve so much for the poor woman whose earthly sufferings are now at an end. Time is a great healer, and you will soon find a new purpose in life and learn to be happy again."

He looked at me strangely, and then replied: "How can I be happy again when I have but one more day to live, brother?"

"Don't think such desperate thoughts," I begged him. "You are still fit and well, and you have many years of life to look forward to."

"I see I must explain the custom of our land," he said quietly. "Here, if the wife dies first her husband is buried alive in the same grave with her."

I could scarcely believe it, and was beginning to protest that it was the most barbarous and uncivilized custom that I had ever heard of, when a crowd of comforters arrived and fell to commiserating with my friend on the death of his wife.

Then they laid the dead woman out and, setting her on a bier, carried her in procession through the city, being sure to take her wretched husband with them.

They bore her to a rocky promontory by the sea, where they rolled back a large stone to reveal a shaft into which they deposited the body. Then, after tying a rope under the husband's armpits, they lowered him down the shaft into the cavern below and, with him, a great pitcher of water and seven small loaves.

When he reached the bottom he untied himself from the rope
and they hauled it up again and blocked the opening to the pit
with the large stone. Then the mourners slowly processed back to
the city, leaving my poor friend in the cavern with his dead wife.

At the first opportunity I asked the King why it had been absolutely necessary for the wretched husband to meet this cruel death.

"It is the custom of the country," said the King. "It has been so from time immemorial. If the husband dies first the wife is buried with him; if the wife dies first the husband is buried with her. Thus, we never put asunder man and wife, neither in life nor in death."

I thought for a moment, and then cleared my throat and asked, casually: "And if the wife of a foreigner were to die before her husband, what then?"

"We should deal with him in exactly the same way as we have dealt with our late-lamented friend," replied the King, placidly helping himself to a sweetmeat.

At this I felt my heart pounding in my chest and the blood pumping in my ears. My eyes clouded over as though I were already imprisoned in a dark, airless dungeon.

This thought haunted my mind for weeks, and I began to fear and hate the society in which I found myself. My mind was obsessed with the idea that my wife might die before me, and I had constantly to reassure myself that I was much more likely to be the first and that, in any case, if I took her back to my own home we should be well out of the reach of this inhuman law.

As Fate would have it, my wife was taken ill not long after this and, after a few days' lingering on her sickbed, passed away. Intending nothing but kindness, our friends and relations came to the house to offer me their condolences on the death of my wife—and also on my impending departure from this world.

The constant attendance of mourners made escape impossible:

there were people sitting with me at every moment of the day. The womenfolk came to wash the body of my wife and dress her in her richest garments and golden ornaments. Then they laid her on the bier.

On the fateful day she was borne in procession to the mountain promontory where I had to watch the stone being rolled back and her body being cast into the pit. As the mourners closed in on me to clasp my hands for the last time and to commiserate with me, I begged them to absolve me, a stranger to their land, from such a barbaric custom. I reasoned with them that I would never have consented to be married to her if I had known about the custom in the first place, but they merely nodded sympathetically as they tied the rope around my body and eased me into the void.

When I reached the bottom, with my pitcher of water and my seven loaves of bread, they called down to me to release myself from the rope so that they could draw it up again. This I refused to do, so they simply dropped it down and closed the hole up with the heavy stone.

Peering about, I could make out that I was in a vast cave full of dead bodies, and the air was heavy with the groans of the dying. All I could think of was my utter folly in submitting to being married in a foreign city and for allowing myself, yet again, to escape one set of misfortunes only to encounter something far worse.

"I deserve everything that has ever happened to me!" I cried in misery, beating my breast. "If only I had died a decent death by drowning at sea!"

Then I flung myself down among the bones that covered the floor and lay there sobbing until the pangs of hunger and the fires of thirst roused me to take a little bread and sip a little water.

Groping my way across the cave, I found a ledge in the hollow of the rock, away from any human remains, and there settled myself to what sleep I could manage.

How much time passed I am unable to say, but I do know that eventually I found myself down to the last sip of water and the last crust of bread.

And then, suddenly, there came the sound of the great stone being rolled back, and a shaft of bright daylight streamed into the cave. First a dead woman's body was lowered down, and after that her living husband, who was about my own age.

The unfortunate man crawled to a corner of the cave and lay there without moving. I watched for a long time, and when eventually I dared to approach him I found that he too was now dead.

Some time later I found an explanation to his death. An epidemic of some fatal disease must have ravaged the city, because many more bodies were lowered into the cave, and their

doomed companions survived only a short time. What was unfortunate for them was fortunate for me, because they left me plentiful supplies of bread and water.

Then one day I was awakened by the sound of something scratching in the dark among the bodies in a corner of the cave. Seizing a bone to protect myself, I rose to my feet. Although I feared that it might be wolves or hyenas, or something even worse, I felt that I had to investigate.

When the creature heard me it ran off to the further end of the cave, and I could tell by its scampering that it was only a small beast. Feeling certain that there must be a way out, I made up my mind to follow it.

Hesitantly, I followed the sound until there came a point where I could make out a speck of light in the distance. After a while I found it getting larger and larger until it took the shape of a crevice in the rock wall. On examining it more closely, I came to the conclusion that it was a natural fissure in the rock that had been enlarged by creatures hungry to make a meal of the bodies in the cave.

With a little effort I was able to scramble through the gap. I found myself on the steep slope of a cliff-face, overlooking a remote beach and the salt sea beyond. Once more I had reason to thank my good fortune.

Returning to the cave, I quickly made sacks out of some of the richest of the robes I had removed from the corpses and put into them the best of the gold and silver trinkets and gems and other valuables I had collected. Then I gathered up a quantity of food and water, slipped some of the finer garments over my own, and slung my sacks over my shoulder.

I resolved to wait patiently on the mountainside until Fate should send along some ship to rescue me. I was confident that I had only to revisit the cave every so often to be assured of a constant supply of fresh food and drinking water.

And then one gusty day, when the sea was afoam with dashing billows, I spotted a ship in the distance. Running back into the cave to get a white shroud, I made a banner with a stick and clambered down to the shore, waving it wildly as I went.

When the ship drew nearer I could hear the crew calling to me. "Who are you? And how do you come to be on this mountain where we have never seen sign of human life before?"

Above the noise of the sea I made it be understood that I was a gentleman and a merchant, and that thanks to Destiny—and my own strength and skill and effort—I had saved myself and some of my merchandise after having been shipwrecked on this shore.

They sent a small boat to pick me up with my many bundles, and rowed me back to the ship. There the captain greeted me kindly but he, too, expressed amazement that I should have been on that inaccessible side of the island where, hitherto, he had only ever seen wild beasts and seabirds.

I thought it prudent to say nothing of the cave for fear that among the members of the crew there might be a native of the city. However, I repeated the story of my earlier shipwreck to him in great detail.

Then I took out some of the best of the precious stones and pearls that I had collected and offered them to him for having saved my life, explaining that I had no ready money about me.

"It is our custom and our duty," he replied graciously, "whenever we find a shipwrecked man, to take him up and to feed and clothe him. Far from accepting money from him, we set him ashore at a convenient port of safety, with a gift of money from ourselves."

I thanked him most humbly for his great kindness and undertook to pray for his long life.

The sea journey did something to relieve me of the memory of the horrors I had experienced in the cave. We called in at the Island of the Bell, where there is a city so vast that it takes a man two days to walk from one side to the other. Six days later we reached the Island of Kala, which is ruled over by a powerful king and is famous for its fine camphor, Indian rattan palms (from which they make excellent cane), and lead mines.

At last we landed at Basra and within no time I was back home among all my relatives and friends. I stored away all the precious goods I had brought back with me and distributed alms to all the unfortunates of the city.

And then I gave myself up once more to my old pleasure-loving ways.

And that is the story of my fourth voyage. Tomorrow I shall tell you the story of my fifth.

* * *

After this, the evening meal was served to the guests and Sinbad the Sailor gave his customary purse of a hundred gold dinars to Sinbad the Porter.

Sinbad the Porter's mind was so full of the adventures he had heard that he could hardly sleep that night. The next morning he was up bright and early to be among the first of the guests to arrive to hear the story of The Fifth Voyage of Sinbad the Sailor.

# THE FIFTH VOYAGE

## OF SINBAD THE SAILOR

ONCE again my life of uninterrupted pleasure soon made me forget all the dangers and suffering I had endured on my voyages, and finally my urge to travel to foreign parts seized me with all its previous force.

I used my experience to buy the most appropriate equipment and goods for my journey and had it transported to Basra. There, in the port, I discovered a brand-new boat that took my fancy so much that I bought her on the spot. I then hired a skilled master and crew, above whom I set certain of my stewards as overseers. A number of rich merchants offered me money to take them and their goods, which I accepted, and I immediately gave orders to set sail.

We journeyed from city to city and island to island, selling and buying profitably, until one day we arrived at a desolate island on the shore of which could be seen a white dome-shaped object, half-buried in the sand.

While I was attending to necessary matters on board ship, the merchants landed and began to investigate the dome. Not knowing what it was, they began striking it with stones to discover what was inside. It was, in fact, a Roc's egg, and they soon broke the shell with their stones. Water gushed from the egg, revealing a baby Roc inside.

At once the merchants decided to light a fire and make a meal of the bird, to which purpose they began struggling to pull it out of the shell. One of the crew, seeing this, immediately reported the matter to me which, of course, filled me with horror.

"For pity's sake leave the egg alone and return to the ship," I called, "or the great Roc will see you attacking its young and will attack us in return! I order you to come back on board before it is too late!"

But it seemed it *was* too late. The sun darkened as the male Roc's mighty wings blotted out the light. The bird circled the little group on the shore, making angry cries. Alerted by its calls, its mate appeared and the two of them wheeled overhead, sending the merchants scampering back to the ship in panic.

And then, to my relief, the Rocs decided to fly away, but my instinct told me to cast off at once and make for the open sea. My instinct was correct. Soon after, the Rocs reappeared, each carrying an enormous boulder in its claws. The male Roc was the first to drop his boulder, but it narrowly missed us, although the force

with which it hit the water was enough to send the ship pitching
and tossing madly. Almost before we could recover, the female
Roc let fall her boulder, which crashed through the poop of the
ship, splintering the rudder into twenty pieces.

The vessel foundered and we were all flung into the sea. Good
fortune was once more on my side: a plank from the ship was
within arm's reach, and I grabbed hold of it and managed to
straddle it, paddling with my feet until the winds and the waves
threw me up on the shore of another island.

When I had recovered sufficiently to take stock of my new surroundings, I was relieved to find that Fate had cast me up on a most delightful shore. The trees were weighed down with fruits of all descriptions and the air was scented with a profusion of flowers. So I ate my fill and drank from the cool streams and sank, exhausted, into a deep sleep.

The next morning, refreshed, I explored a little further. Supposing the island to be totally uninhabited, I was surprised to come upon a very old man, wearing a palm-frond waistcloth, sitting alone by a spring.

I assumed that he must be one of the merchants who had also survived the shipwreck and saluted him and wished him well. He returned my greeting with a sign of his hands but uttered not a word.

"Venerable sir," I said, "what causes you to sit here, and how can I be of help?" He shook his head pathetically and made a sign as if to ask me to take him upon my shoulders and carry him across the stream.

Having pity on the aged man, I willingly crouched down, hoisted him on my shoulders, and stepped across the stream. There I crouched again to allow him to dismount from my shoulders. But instead, he wrapped his legs tightly around my neck.

When I looked more closely and saw that they were as dark and rough as buffalo's hide, I felt alarmed and tried to shake him off, but he gripped even more tightly until I found it hard to breathe and felt my head swimming.

And then, having shown me who was master, he made signals with his hands and squeezed and kicked with his legs to indicate that I should carry him from one tree to another to allow him to pluck the best fruits. If I misunderstood an instruction, or moved too slowly from tiredness, or lost my footing and stumbled, he would drum his feet into my ribs, making me cry out in pain.

For days and nights I had to undergo this torture. At no time did he get down from my shoulders. At night, when he felt tired, he would give the signal for us to stretch out on the ground, but even in sleep he kept his legs tightly locked around my throat. When he was ready to move in the morning he would rouse me with a beating from his heels that was ten times more painful than palm rods.

I cursed myself again and deeply repented having taken pity on this vile creature, and vowed that I would never do another good deed for any man as long as I lived. My life was so wretched that there were times when I honestly wished I might be able to die, but still I wearily dragged on.

Then one day I had an idea to relieve my existence of a little of its misery. I had been commanded to halt at a spot where there were many vines and gourds, some of them quite dry. While the old man was busy picking fruits, I plucked a great dry gourd, wrenched off the top, scooped out the inside and cleaned it, and then gathered some grapes and squeezed them into the gourd until it was full of juice. Then I plugged the mouth of the gourd and left it hanging in the sun.

Several days later, when we were passing that way again, I took the opportunity to take a sip of the liquid: it had become strong wine and was most refreshing. Every time we passed that spot I would taste a little, to ease my aches and pains.

Then, one day, the old man looked down and noticed me drinking. Angrily he drummed with his heels and waved with his arms as if to demand, "What are you doing that for?" I tried to explain that the wine made me feel happier, and to show him what I meant I took another swig and began to dance with him on my shoulders, weaving among the trees and clapping my hands and singing.

At once he wanted to try it for himself, so I had no choice but to hand him the gourd. It pleased him so much that he drank it down to the last drop and immediately began to feel light-headed. He started to sway violently and clap his hands.

At last he became so drunk that I could feel his muscles relaxing around my neck. Seizing the opportunity, I grabbed hold of his legs and flung him backwards off my shoulders, hardly able to believe my good luck. When I looked around I saw that, in his fall, his head had struck a large rock. He was dead.

Then, feeling much more at ease than I had felt for a long time, I returned to the beach to keep a lookout for ships in the distance.

Many days passed, but at last a ship arrived and some passengers landed. When they saw me they wanted to know how I came to be on that remote island, and I told them everything that had happened since I had set sail from Basra.

They told me how fortunate I was to have escaped alive from my last encounter. It seems that I had met The Old Man of the Sea and that no one who had felt his legs around their neck had ever survived: they had all died of exhaustion beneath him, and then he had eaten their wasted bodies.

Then, congratulating me again on my good fortune, they offered me something to eat and drink and gave me some fresh clothes (which I was badly in need of) and took me aboard their ship.

After many days, we landed at a place they called the City of Apes. It had many imposing houses, all of which faced the sea, and it had a single gate studded with iron nails. It was explained to me that every evening at dusk the inhabitants came out of the gate and put to sea in boats, passing the night on the water for fear of being attacked by apes from the mountain.

Although I had every reason to be wary of the ape-kind, I ventured on land to inspect the city, since it was still broad daylight. But, to my great distress, the ship sailed off without me. It seemed that, yet again, I was the author of my own misfortunes.

Luckily one of the townsfolk, identifying me as a stranger, came out to greet me and to offer help. When he heard that I had been stranded, he immediately offered me a spare place in his boat. "For if you remain here at night," he said, "the apes will be sure to kill you."

And so I spent the night in the safety of his boat, about one mile out to sea, and in the morning we rowed back to the city with all the other little boats. I learned that at daybreak, having eaten what they could of the produce of the gardens, the apes always went back to their mountains until the following night.

Another of the townsfolk, taking pity on my plight, asked me if I had any trade or profession that I could practice while I was waiting for another ship to take me home. When I told him that I was a merchant and a man of some substance who, until just recently, had owned his own ship, he handed me a cotton bag.

"Take this bag and fill it with pebbles from the beach," he said, "and then join the small band of townsfolk to whom I shall introduce you. Do exactly what they do and I guarantee that you shall earn your daily bread and not go home empty-handed."

He escorted me down to the beach, where I collected my pebbles, and then he entrusted me to the care of a little group of townsfolk, all of whom were carrying similar cotton bags. They gave me a friendly welcome and took me with them to a broad riverbed where there were some tall trees with trunks so smooth that no human could climb them.

There were many apes sleeping in the shade of these trees, and when they heard us approaching they swarmed up the trees to take shelter among the topmost branches. I then noticed that my companions were opening their bags and taking out pebbles.

To my surprise they began to throw these pebbles at the apes. And, to my greater surprise, the angry apes began to retaliate by picking the coconuts off the trees and throwing them down at us. Of course, we began to pick up the nuts, and even before I had used up all the pebbles in my bag, my companions and I had gathered as many coconuts as we could carry.

Back in the city, I went to the house of the friendly man who had presented me to the group and offered him the valuable nuts, but he declined graciously and gave me some good advice.

"Make this your trade until you can return home," he said. "Every day go out with your pebbles and bring your coconuts back here to leave in my storehouse, for which I shall give you a key. Sell and use for yourself the very ripest; the others, with good fortune, you can trade with on your return home." And he wished me luck.

And so every day I went out with the coconut gatherers and did good business in the market. By occupying myself in this way I enjoyed my stay in the city. But all the same I was glad when a ship eventually put in at the port and I was able to arrange a passage back to my homeland.

I thanked my friend for all his kindnesses, and embarked with my new merchandise in high spirits.

We sailed from island to island and sea to sea, and everywhere we went I bartered profitably. One of the islands we visited was famed for its cloves and cinnamon and pepper, all of which I bought in great quantities.

I was told how, beside each cluster of pepper berries, there grows a great leaf that shades it from the sun and protects it from the water in the rainy season, but then droops down when it is no longer needed.

We also called in at the Island of Al-Usirat where the Cape Comorin aloe wood comes from, and also at another very long island, five days' journey from one end to the other, which produces even better aloe wood than the Comorin, but unfortunately the inhabitants are a foul, immoral lot.

From there we visited some pearl fisheries where I presented some of the divers with coconuts, saying "Dive, and bring me good luck!" And indeed they did, fetching me up a great store of priceless pearls from the depths of the lagoon.

Finally I got back to Basra, and thence to Baghdad, where once more I gathered all my friends and relatives about me to celebrate my safe return. I could afford to make generous presents to all, and distributed alms among the poor.

And that is the story of my fifth voyage. Tomorrow I shall tell you the story of my sixth.

* * *

Then, after they had all feasted, Sinbad the Sailor gave Sinbad the Porter a purse of a hundred gold dinars, bidding him to be sure to return in good time the following day.

The next morning the two men talked together until all the other guests had arrived and food had been passed around. And then began the story of The Sixth Voyage of Sinbad the Sailor.

# THE SIXTH VOYAGE

## OF SINBAD THE SAILOR

ILIVED a life of great ease and luxury after my return from my fifth voyage, quite forgetting all the ordeals I had been through. Life seemed perfect until one day I offered hospitality to a company of merchants. No sooner had they begun to tell me of their adventures in foreign lands, and of the sheer delight in trading in exotic goods, than my soul ached to be sailing the seven seas again.

By now I was experienced in buying the fine wares necessary for such a voyage and I soon found myself in Basra once more, embarking on a sturdy ship with other wealthy merchants.

We set sail in good spirits, travelling from city to city and island to island, trading at a handsome profit and entertaining ourselves with the strange sights. Fortune smiled upon us for some time.

But one day the captain flung his turban on the deck and raised his arms above his head with a great wail. Then he plucked at his beard, clasped his hands over his face, and fell to his knees crying, "Alas, alas, that my children should be orphaned at such a tender age!"

In alarm we clustered around him, begging him to tell us what the trouble was. It was as though the brightness had turned to threatening dark in a split second. At last he regained his composure sufficiently to raise his head and address us.

"Good sirs," he said in a hushed voice, "the dreadful truth is that we have wandered far off course and have drifted into uncharted waters. Unless Fortune quickly offers us a means of escape, we are as good as dead. Fall to your prayers!"

With that, he clambered up the mast to see if there was help at hand, and he would have loosed the sails if a violent wind had not come up at that moment and whirled the ship around and back, driving her onto some rocks and breaking the rudder.

"No man can escape that which Fate has ordained for him," wailed the captain, descending the mast, which set many of the merchants tearing their robes and weeping and bidding each other a last farewell.

I just had time to see that the rocks were the outcrop of a huge mountain that rose from the sea, when the ship was buffeted against some more, breaking up on the impact and flinging us all into the seething waters. Many drowned, but together with some of the other merchants, I had the good luck to be flung up on the rugged shore.

From the base of the mountain I could make out that we were on a bleak peninsula, the lower slopes of which were strewn with the wreckage of ships and merchandise and gear that the sea had cast up. The merchants who had survived were scurrying towards the abandoned treasures like men possessed, but I decided to go my own way.

Scrambling up the lower cliffs, I found a track through them to the rocky interior. Not far ahead of me I saw a stream that seemed to well up from the mountain face and then disappear into the rocks again a little way beyond. Imagine my amazement when I bent down to refresh myself with this clear water and saw, lying on the bed of the stream like so many pebbles, a wealth of rubies and pearls and jewels and precious stones of every kind. The very sands at the edge of the rivulet sparkled and glistened with gems and precious ores.

Venturing further, I saw that the peninsula had an abundance of aloe wood (of both the Chinese and the Comorin varieties) and that there was also a spring of pure ambergris that flowed like wax or gum, owing to the great heat of the sun, right down to the shore, where sea monsters would emerge to swallow it before plunging into the depths again. But it burns their bellies so much that they have to regurgitate it, and it then congeals on the surface of the water, undergoing a change in hue and texture. Finally, it gets thrown up on the beach to be collected by travellers and merchants, who prize it highly.

Not all the ambergris flowed down to the sea: some of it trickled through the fields in little rivulets, here and there settling on the banks where it melted in the sun, giving the whole valley a musk-like fragrance. But because the mountain appears so forbidding, no travellers, it seems, had ever found their way to this remarkable source.

When I rejoined my companions on the rocky shores, our first talk was of the marvels of the place, but then our thoughts turned to our sorry plight and we at once set about scavenging what little food we could from the debris on the beach. It was little enough, and although for the following days we rationed it out scrupulously, nearly everyone was weak from colic and seasickness, and many of them died. We washed and shrouded them in clothes and linen that had been cast up on the shore, and buried them as best we could.

Once again, Fate protected me but, finally, there came the sorry day when I was left to bury the last remaining one of my companions, and had to face the grim prospect of life all alone in this desolate spot. To think that I, who had once had so much, should be left to survive on so little. "If only I had died sooner," I thought; "far better that than die miserably by myself, with no one to wash and bury *me*."

With that thought haunting my mind I took a spade that had been cast ashore and dug myself a shallow grave. When the time came that I felt myself growing weak, I would be able to fling myself into it and die there, knowing that the drifting sand would soon cover my dead body and give me a decent burial. And then I cursed myself again for having been so foolish, after all the hardships I had undergone in my first five voyages, as to leave the comforts of my native land for the unknown hazards of yet another sea voyage.

At home I had more money than I could ever have hoped to spend in a lifetime, and now, in my mad quest for more, I had thrown away the chance of ever enjoying it again.

As I sat there bemoaning my stupidity, my gaze fell on the fresh-water stream once more. It occurred to me that it must go somewhere and that it might flow past some inhabited place in the course of its journey. So I set about constructing a little raft from pieces of aloe wood that I bound together with ropes from the wreckage. Then I selected some driftwood planks of even size that I lashed to the base to form a solid platform, just narrow enough to travel down the stream.

After that, I loaded it with merchandise and precious stones and ambergris from the beach, together with the remains of the food and some wild herbs. Lastly, I selected two lengths of wood to serve as oars and launched the raft off, thinking, "Nothing ventured, nothing gained," as the proverb has it.

I let the raft drift for a little while until I came to a point where the stream disappeared into the mountain through a small opening. In the dark I could feel the raft scraping along the sides of the rock walls, and soon I had to lie on my stomach to stop my head from bumping against the roof. It occurred to me that if the tunnel were to get any narrower my raft would be stuck, and there would be no way of rowing back against the current.

After hours of slow progress, my senses were confused by the fatigue, the darkness, and the fear of becoming trapped, and I lost consciousness. How long I drifted face-down on my raft I have no idea, but when I opened my eyes once more I found that it was broad daylight and that I was lying on my back in a meadow. Looking around, I saw that my raft was moored to a small island, where it was being inspected closely by a number of Indians and Abyssinians.

When one of them noticed that I was awake, they all came across to me and immediately began gabbling in their different languages. Not understanding a word that was being said, and still feeling rather light-headed from the dark tunnel and lack of food, I half-wondered if I were still asleep and dreaming.

Seeing how bewildered I looked, one of them tried addressing me in Arabic, asking how I had come to make such a journey since no one had ever reached them from the other side of the mountain. I was delighted to be able to answer his question, and begged him to tell me where I was.

"Friend," he said, "we are simple toilers of the land, and when we came out to water our crops this morning we found you asleep on your raft and gently carried you to rest in the field." And then he asked for more details about my adventure.

But first I begged him for something to eat, which he provided willingly. Feeling much refreshed after my meal, I was able to satisfy their curiosity with a detailed account of my experiences, at which they all wondered and then conferred together.

Finally they decided that I had recovered sufficiently to be presented to their monarch, the King of Sarandib. So they took me and the raft, still laden with its merchandise, gemstones, and ambergris, to the royal palace, where my Arab interpreter explained to the King how I came to be in their country.

The King entreated me to repeat my story from beginning to end, and when I had finished he wished me well on my safe deliverance and said that it had been a remarkable adventure indeed.

After this, I requested that a great store of precious ores and jewels and ambergris should be brought from the raft, and this I presented as a gift to the King, who gratefully received it and begged that I would accept lodging in the palace as his guest. And so it was that I became acquainted with the most distinguished of his subjects.

I was free to explore to my heart's content, and I soon discovered that the Island of Sarandib, which has a day and night each measuring twelve hours, is eighty leagues long and thirty across, being divided by a high mountain and a deep valley. This mountain is visible from a distance of three days and contains many kinds of rubies and other precious stones and spice trees of every variety. The surface of it is covered with emery, which is used to cut and fashion gems. The riverbeds are strewn with diamonds and the valleys with pearls. I climbed to the top of the mountain and spent hours wondering at its marvels, which are truly indescribable. Then I returned to the King.

Whenever travellers and merchants came to pay their respects at the palace, I was introduced to them, to be questioned on my native land and how Caliph Harun al-Rashid ruled his state. I told them of his wisdom and merits and, in turn, asked them about the customs of their own countries.

As the King heard more about the Caliph's manner of governing, he grew more and more impressed. "Indeed," he said one day, "you are blessed with a wise and praiseworthy ruler, and your description of him fills me with the deepest respect. I shall make him a gift and you shall deliver it to him." I was overjoyed to hear this and assured the King that I would sing his praises to the Caliph.

In fact, I stayed with the King for a considerable time after this, receiving numerous gifts from him, until one day word reached me that a company of merchants was fitting out a ship for Basra and I realized that this was my opportunity to return home and perform the King's mission.

I immediately told the King what I had discovered and requested his permission to secure a passage on the ship. "You are, and ever shall be, your own master," he said, graciously. "And yet, you know that if you desire to stay here with us, it will be my pleasure and my privilege to provide for you."

I thanked him with all my heart and assured him that, although I was overwhelmed by his kindness and generosity, I pined deeply for my home and my friends. When the King heard this he bestowed great riches from his treasury upon me and entrusted me with a magnificent present for Caliph Harun al-Rashid. He also gave me a sealed letter, entreating me to bear it with my own hand to the Commander of the Faithful with all appropriate salutations.

"To hear is to obey," I replied, and took the letter from him. It was written on parchment made from the skin of the khawi, which is yellow and far finer than lambskin parchment, and the ink was of ultramarine. The message greeted the Caliph in peace and friendship, described some of the marvels of the King's palace and estates, and begged him to accept the trifling gift—though unworthy of him—as a gesture of brotherliness.

The trifling gift consisted of a cup carved from a ruby a span high, decorated inside with precious pearls; a bed, covered with the spotted skin of a serpent that swallowed elephants, which had the power to protect from ill health anyone who reclined on it; and a hundred thousand miskals of aloe wood.

Then the King summoned the master of the ship and the merchants and commended me to their care, paying for my freight and for my passage. After taking a touching leave of him and my acquaintances, I embarked and we set sail for Basra.

Fortune smiled on us and we made good speed. As quickly as I could after reaching Basra, I made for Baghdad and the Caliph's palace, where I sought an audience in the King's name. I bowed low, had the King's presents laid out before him, and handed him the letter. The Caliph was full of amazement.

"But is what the King writes really true?" he asked.

"Oh, my lord," I replied, "with my own eyes I saw sights far exceeding anything he writes of in that letter. For state processions a throne is set for him on the back of a huge elephant, eleven cubits high; and he sits on this throne with his great lords and officers and attendants standing in two ranks to his right and to his left. Before this throne is an officer bearing a gold javelin, and immediately behind the throne is another bearing a great gold mace, the head of which is an emerald as thick as a man's thumb.

"And when he rides out on horseback he is accompanied by a thousand horsemen clad in gold brocade and silk. Before him

rides an officer proclaiming his greatness and power and dignity; while behind him rides another crying out, 'But he will die; he will surely die.'

"Moreover, by the shining example he sets to all, there are no justices needed in the city; all his subjects know right from wrong and live accordingly."

The Caliph praised the King for his wisdom, and summoned his scribes to take down all I could tell the court about my experiences in that remarkable country. Then he conferred handsome gifts upon me and gave me leave to return to my own house.

There I distributed gifts to my relatives and friends and gave alms to the poor and unfortunate, and soon forgot the hardships that I had endured as I rediscovered the taste for the life of luxury and indulgence.

And that is the story of my sixth voyage. Tomorrow I shall tell you the story of my seventh, which is even more amazing than the first six.

\* \* \*

Then, at his bidding, the company feasted into the small hours, and he gave Sinbad the Porter his usual purse of a hundred gold dinars. After that they all went their ways, marvelling at what they had heard.

When Sinbad the Porter arrived the next morning, the guests were already assembling to hear the story of The Seventh Voyage of Sinbad the Sailor.

# THE
# SEVENTH VOYAGE

## OF SINBAD THE SAILOR

IMMEDIATELY after my return from my sixth voyage, as I said, I resumed my old way of life, enjoying the good things in life in the company of friends.

But little by little my soul began to yearn once more for the excitement of the sea and foreign parts. I had my bales packed and made for Basra, where I chanced upon a fine ship just ready to sail. I found myself among a crowd of wealthy merchants and soon made the acquaintance of them all.

The wind was fair and the voyage promised to be a prosperous one until we left the city of Madinat-al-Sin. We were gathered on deck, enthusiastically discussing our successful trading ventures, when out of nowhere, a violent headwind blew up and the heavens opened, drenching us with rain.

While we were frantically covering our bales with our cloaks and canvas to prevent our goods from being ruined, the ship's master appeared, tucked up his skirts in his girdle, and shinned up the mast. We watched as he looked to the left and to the right, and then we saw him pummel his brow and pluck at his beard like a man distracted.

We began to grow alarmed and begged him to tell us what the matter was. He clambered down, urging us to say our final prayers and bid each other farewell, because the wind had got the better of the ship and had driven us to the furthermost point of the ocean.

Then, opening his sea chest, he pulled out a blue cotton bag from which he took some ash-like powder. He sprinkled this into a saucer moistened with water, waited a short time, and then tasted and smelled it. After that he consulted an old book, muttering as he did so: "Alas, this work foretells of certain disaster, for this is the Sea of the Clime of the King where lies the sepulchre of King Solomon, and all around are fearsome sea monsters. Whenever a ship has the ill-luck to drift into these waters, a sea monster is sure to rise from the depths and swallow her up, with everyone on board."

We were terrified by the captain's words, but more terrified still when there came a loud rumble like thunder and there rose ahead of us a mountainous sea monster of gruesome appearance. We had all fallen to our prayers when another, even larger and more hideous than the first, broke through the water. But we were paralyzed with horror as the third and biggest bore down upon us with gaping jaws, threatening to swallow us.

Its open mouth was like the gates of a city and its throat was like a long, dark tunnel. But just at the moment when it seemed that we would be sucked in, a violent squall arose, flinging the ship upon a great reef, where it smashed into pieces, hurling all of us into the sea.

I managed to tear off my outer garments and clutched a plank that was being tossed about in the seething water. At last I got astride it and let the wind and waves buffet me where they would. Distressed and weary, I lamented the weakness of my will. How many times had I told myself that I must renounce the hazards of the sea; and how many times had I lied to myself that I would.

"I can blame no one, not even Fate," I wailed. "I truly deserve everything I suffer." And for the first time I sincerely repented my greed for wealth, and vowed never even to dream of travel again were it granted me to return safely home once more.

The winds and waves bore me on for two days, until I was finally cast up on a great island covered in luxuriant growth and abounding with clear streams. When I had refreshed myself with water and fruit, I sat down and reflected that, whatever misfortunes I had undergone in my travels, Fate had usually smiled on me in the end.

Then I began to explore and soon found myself beside a broad and swift-flowing river. Recalling how I had saved myself by constructing a raft on my last adventure, I resolved to make another. I reasoned that if I perished in the strong current, at least that would put a certain end to my ordeal.

So I set about gathering a supply of large pieces of wood from the trees, which were—though I was unaware of this at the time—the very finest sandalwood, and I twisted creepers into

lengths of rope with which I secured the logs together. Then, committing myself to Fate, I launched my raft into mid-stream.

The powerful current swept me along for three days and nights, with only a little fruit to sustain me and only the river water to slake my thirst. By the beginning of the fourth day I was weak and giddy from apprehension and hunger.

My fear increased when, looking ahead, I saw that the river disappeared into a high mountain. Remembering my previous ordeal in a narrow subterranean passage, I did all I could to grab at overhanging branches to prevent myself from being swept through the tunnel opening. But the current was far too powerful and I was hurled headlong on my raft straight into the dark hole.

Mercifully, the journey through the tunnel was brief, and soon I found myself emerging into the open air. Below me was a kind of valley into which the river plunged with a noise like rolling thunder. I gripped the sides of the raft for dear life and scarcely dared to open my eyes. Little by little the current eased, but I still couldn't muster enough strength or resolution to try to direct my craft towards the riverbank.

Eventually I found that I was being carried towards the port of a vast and imposing city. When the crowd saw me approaching, they hailed me and threw ropes from the quays. But I was too exhausted to be able to grab them, and so they cast a net over the raft and drew it ashore. They had to lift me off, for all the world like a dead man.

Then an aged man of reverend appearance edged his way through the crowd, bowed courteously, and threw a robe around my shoulders. He entreated me to accompany him to the bathhouse, where he commanded the attendants to warm me back to life and to bathe me in fragrant perfumes and to set delicious sherbet drinks before me.

After that they dressed me in rich garments and led me to the old man's house. There I was welcomed as a special guest and offered all manner of delicacies. His pages fetched me hot water to wash my hands in and his handmaids brought me silken napkins.

Then the master of the house told me that an apartment had been prepared for me and that his servants had been instructed to provide for my every need. I thanked him humbly and enjoyed his generous hospitality for three days, in which time my fears abated and my mind was completely eased.

On the fourth day the master came into my guest chamber and said, "It delights my heart, my son, to see you restored so soon. Let us go down to the bazaar together to sell your stock. It will command a high price and, for I assume you are a merchant, will provide you with the means of buying some useful and valuable merchandise to trade with. I have already commanded my servants to retrieve your goods for you."

At this I was totally bewildered. "I thank you for your concern, sir," I said, "but what goods have I, an unfortunate shipwrecked man, to trade with?"

"I see you are still somewhat confused after your ordeal," he said sympathetically. "But come with me to the bazaar, and if any trader makes a reasonable offer, let us accept it; if not, permit me to take the goods into my warehouse until such times as they will bring a fairer price."

Out of curiosity, and in order not to upset my kind host, I agreed to accompany him to the marketplace where, to my astonishment, I saw an eager crowd of rich-looking merchants gathered around the pieces of my dismantled raft.

My host's agent was calling out that this was sandalwood of the finest quality, the like of which had never been offered for sale in those parts. The bidding opened briskly and didn't stop until an offer of one thousand dinars was made.

At this my host turned to me and said, "This is a fair price in hard times like this. Are you content to accept it, or would you prefer me to lay up the wood in my storehouse until times are easier?" I could only say that I would take his advice in all matters.

"In that case, my son," he said, "would you sell the wood to me at a price a hundred gold pieces above that offered by the last bidder?" I was overcome by emotion. "Only if you feel that it is suitable that I can accept any payment at all from someone who has already been generous beyond the call of duty," I said. He smiled courteously and ordered his servants to carry off the wood to his warehouse. Then he escorted me back to his house and counted out the money into separate bags, which he then placed in a small, private chamber that he made fast with an iron padlock. He put the key into my hands.

Some days later the old sheikh told me that he had a proposal to make to me that he dearly hoped I would accept. "I am advanced in years," he said, "and I have no son. But I do have a young and beautiful daughter, who is both gifted and wealthy. It would gladden my heart if you would accept her hand in marriage and live here with us in this country. I will hand over all my business affairs to you and make you master of the house in my place."

I could not answer. I was too overcome with embarrassment.

"You shall be as my son," he continued, "and everything that I call mine shall be yours. And if the desire takes you to travel to your own country and trade there, no one shall hinder you."

"You have already become as a father to me, good sir," I said. "But I am a stranger in this land, and the hardships I have undergone in my travels have robbed me of my judgment. It is for you alone to decide what I should do."

He was delighted with this reply and immediately sent for the judge to marry us, and ordered his servants to prepare a magnificent wedding banquet. For my part, I fell in love with his daughter the moment I clapped eyes on her. She had perfect symmetry and grace and, moreover, wore a dazzling profusion of ornaments and necklaces of gold and silver and precious stones.

We lived together in love and harmony. And then, one day, her father passed peacefully away. We shrouded him and buried him, and all his wealth passed to me. The merchants of the city respected my authority as his replacement, for he had been their sheikh and their chief, and no transactions had been carried out without his knowledge and approval.

As a result I became more closely acquainted with the people and their ways. One amazing thing I discovered was that at the beginning of each month the men were transformed: their faces changed and they grew wings. Then they flew into the upper regions of the sky, leaving the city empty except for the women and children.

I decided to ask one of them to take me with him the next month, and when the time came and I met a man undergoing the transformation, I put my request to him.

"Alas, I cannot," he said; but I insisted until he finally gave way. And so, without telling my wife or my servants what I was doing, I clambered astride his back and felt myself rising into the air.

Higher and higher we soared with the other flying men until we reached the point where I could hear the angels singing under the heavenly dome. So excited was I that I called out, "Praise be to the Almighty!" But hardly had the words passed my lips than there came a blast of fire from Heaven and everyone immediately plunged down, cursing me as they went.

My companion, seething with anger, roughly cast me off on the top of a high mountain and abandoned me to my fate. Once again my curiosity had landed me in a dreadful plight. No sooner do I escape one torment than I throw myself into a worse.

As I stood there, not knowing what to do, two young men approached up the mountainside, each as radiant as the moon and each supporting himself with a staff of red gold. I threw myself at their feet with relief and asked who they were.

"We are the servants of the Almighty," they replied, "and we live in these mountains." And, without another word, they presented me with a gold rod and went on their way.

I ventured down the path from which they had appeared, supporting myself on the staff, when suddenly I stumbled upon a serpent that was struggling with a man that it had swallowed up to his navel. When he saw me he cried out that whoever rescued him would be delivered from all adversity. I immediately struck the serpent on the head with the golden staff, at which she spewed the man out of her mouth. Then I struck her a second time and she turned and fled.

"You have saved my life," he said, "and in return I can do you a service by showing you the way down the mountain." I accepted his offer and his company with great relief.

A little way down the mountain we came upon a small company of people, among whom I recognized the man who had carried me on his back and had then abandoned me. Not wishing to upset him further, I approached him and apologized for having inadvertently been the cause of such distress.

He still looked resentful, and told me that I had nearly been the cause of their deaths for praising the Almighty in those regions. I apologized again and begged him to take me once more upon his back and return to the city, on the condition that I would not utter a word. He looked most unhappy but reluctantly agreed.

Then I gave the golden rod to the young man whom I had saved from the serpent, and flew down to the city and my own house, on the back of the other man.

My wife came forward to greet me. But when she had heard my story she looked alarmed.

"You must never fly with these people," she said, "and you must have as little as possible to do with them. For they are the brethren of the demons."

I was astonished and asked how it was that they were all known to her father.

"My father was not one of them," she said. "He came from different parts and his way of life was not theirs. In fact, now that he is dead I realize that it would be far better for you to sell all our possessions and buy goods for trading with on our voyage back to your home country. I feel uneasy living among these people."

So I sold all the sheikh's property, bit by bit, and then sought for any ships that might be sailing to Basra. Soon I heard of a company of merchants who planned to make the voyage but had not been able to find a ship. Eventually they had to buy the materials and build the ship themselves. They were happy to give me a passage when I offered to pay all their expenses.

We set sail from island to island and from sea to sea, and always with a fair wind, so that we arrived at Basra safe and sound. I immediately set out for Baghdad with my wife, stored my goods in my storehouses, and summoned all my relatives and friends to my house.

They all marvelled at my return because, reckoning up the length of time of this my last absence, they calculated that I had been away for twenty-seven years. They were all overjoyed to see me, and listened with wonder to the tales I had to tell. Then, before the assembled company, I solemnly vowed that I would never put to sea again; my seventh voyage had been my last.

\* \* \*

And Sinbad the Sailor turned to Sinbad the Porter and said, "And so you see what sufferings I had to undergo and what dangers I had to face before I came into all this wealth."

"I do indeed," replied Sinbad the Porter, "and I apologize for ever having envied you your good fortune."

And from that time on they were the best of friends, and lived in the pleasure of each other's company until death finally called them.